Written by

JULIA DONALDSON

Illustrated by

LYDIA MONKS

Princess Mirror-Belle

and the Dragon Pox

MACMILLAN CHILDREN'S BOOKS

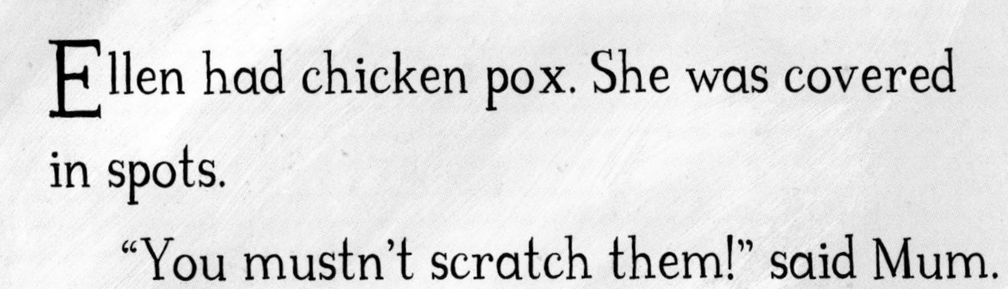

Ellen had chicken pox. She was covered in spots.

"You mustn't scratch them!" said Mum.

Ellen put on her right slipper (she had lost the left one) and went to look at her spots in the bathroom mirror. The spot on her nose was so itchy! Surely a tiny little scratch wouldn't do any harm? Ellen lifted a finger to her nose . . .

Then she jumped, when a voice from the mirror said, "Don't scratch! You might turn into a toad!"

Could this really be happening? Could Ellen's reflection really be talking to her? Before Ellen could reply, the mirror girl went on: "You've got really bad dragon pox."

"No I haven't," said Ellen. "I've got *chicken* pox. And so have you. You're my reflection."

"Don't be silly," said the mirror girl, and the next second she had jumped out of the mirror and was in the bathroom with Ellen. "I'm Princess Mirror-Belle. You really ought to curtsey, but as you're my friend I'll let you off."

"Are you really a princess?" asked Ellen. "But you look just like me. You've got the same pyjamas. You've even lost one of your slippers like me."

"Oh no I haven't," said Mirror-Belle. She paused for a second and then continued: "My slipper was stolen by a goblin. They're always stealing slippers. They like to sleep in them."

Ellen laughed. "Do they have little sheets and pillows?" she asked.

“Never mind that,” said Mirror-Belle. “We need to get started on the cure for dragon pox.” And she put the plug in the bath and turned on the taps.

“But I haven’t got dragon pox,” said Ellen.

“Well, I have,” Mirror-Belle said firmly. “You see, a dragon captured me last week and carried me off to his mountain lair. Luckily a knight came and rescued me, but when I got home I came out in these terrible spots.”

“Did the knight want to marry you?” asked Ellen. But Mirror-Belle seemed not to hear her.

"Now then," said Mirror-Belle. "On with the cure! This stuff looks good." She grabbed a bottle of bubble bath and squirted it into the water. Then, "How odd!" she exclaimed, as hundreds of bubbles appeared.

"Don't you have bubble bath back home?" asked Ellen.

"Certainly not," said Mirror-Belle. "But we do have bubble fish. They're much better. They swim about in the bath and blow thousands of bubbles."

"But isn't the bath water a bit hot for the fish?" asked Ellen.

"Never mind that," said Mirror-Belle. "Let's get in."

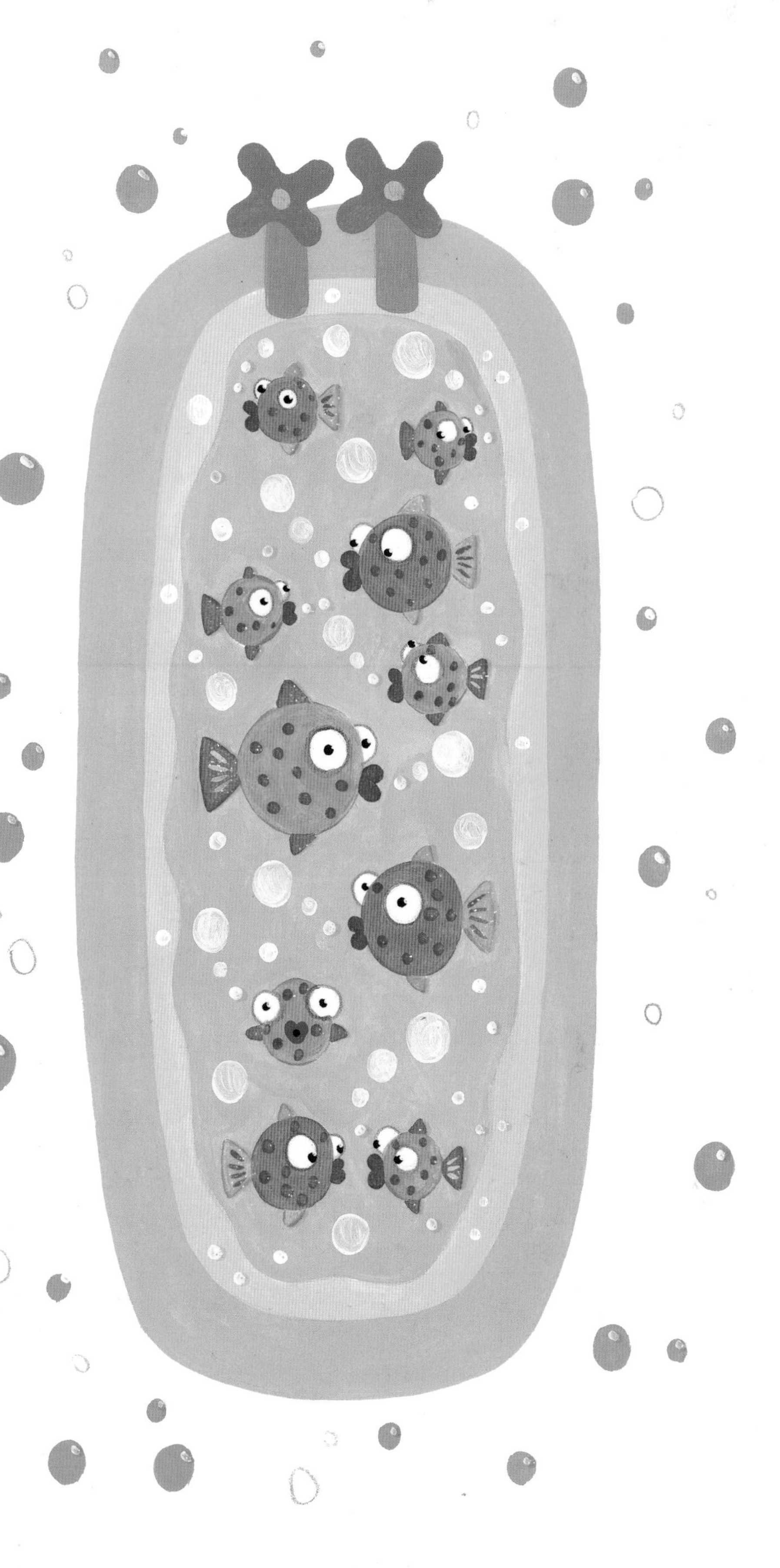

"Hmm, we need some more ingredients," said Mirror-Belle when they were both in the bath. "Let's try this." Before Ellen could stop her, she had squirted a whole tube of toothpaste into the water.

"Hey, now we won't be able to clean our teeth," Ellen protested.

"But can't you get the fairies to clean your teeth?" asked Mirror-Belle.

"No – I don't know any fairies. And what would they use instead of toothpaste?"

"Well, our fairies collect dewdrops from rose petals and use that," said Mirror-Belle.

"How does it stick on the toothbrushes?" asked Ellen.

"I do wish you wouldn't ask so many questions," said Mirror-Belle. "Let's get on with the cure. How about this?" And she squirted in some white foam from a spray can.

"Stop!" cried Ellen. "That's my dad's shaving cream."

"Well, I think he should stop shaving, like my father the King," said Mirror-Belle.

"Does your father have a beard then?" asked Ellen.

"Of course he does. It's so long it reaches the ground. He needs two servants to walk ahead of him to carry it. And sometimes birds make their nests in it."

Ellen laughed. "And do the birds fly in and out feeding worms to their babies?" she asked.

Mirror-Belle didn't reply. Instead, she poured a bottle of shampoo into the bath.

"How will we wash our hair now?" asked Ellen.

"I wouldn't bother washing it," said Mirror-Belle. "When my hair gets dirty I just say a magic spell and wish for some different hair. My hair doesn't always look like yours, you know. Last week I had golden curls and the week before I had . . . er, red ringlets."

"I'd love to do that," said Ellen. "What is the magic spell?"

"I'll tell you later," said Mirror-Belle, and she splashed some frothy creamy foamy toothpasty bath water at Ellen. Ellen giggled and splashed some back. This was beginning to be fun.

But then she noticed that the bathroom floor was getting really wet from all the splashing. "Oh dear, my mum will be a bit cross," she said.

"Really? How peculiar. My mother the Queen is cross if I *don't* splash the floor. In fact she likes me to splash it so much that the whole bathroom is like a paddling pool. Then she paddles about in it to wash her feet, and so do all the palace maids."

"Doesn't the water drip down onto the floor below?" asked Ellen.

"I thought I told you to stop asking questions," said Mirror-Belle. "Now, it's time to get dry and put our pyjamas back on."

"But we're still all spotty," said Ellen as she put on her slipper. "The cure hasn't worked."

"Ah, that's because we haven't done part two yet," said Mirror-Belle.

"What's part two?" asked Ellen.

"This!" Mirror-Belle picked up a roll of loo paper and started to wind it round and round Ellen, who laughed.

"What about you?" she asked.

"We'll do me later," said Mirror-Belle, carrying on winding. Before long Ellen's whole body was covered in loo paper and Mirror-Belle had started on her face.

Then, "Close your eyes and count to a hundred!" she said. So Ellen did.

"... 98, 99, 100!" Ellen ripped the paper off her face and opened her eyes. "Where are you, Mirror-Belle?" she asked.

She looked around the empty room and saw that the door handle was turning.

But it wasn't Mirror-Belle. Instead, Ellen's mum came into the room.

"Ellen, what *have* you been doing?" she said, as she looked at the watery foamy room and all the empty tubes and bottles.

"It wasn't me, it was Princess Mirror-Belle," said Ellen. "She came out of the mirror. She was trying to cure my dragon pox ... I mean, chicken pox."

"Oh, and I suppose she's gone back into the mirror now?" said Ellen's mum.

Ellen looked at the mirror over the basin. It was covered in toothpasty bubbles. "Yes, I think she has," she said.

Ellen's mum sighed. Then she looked at Ellen. "Actually, your spots do look quite a bit better," she said. "That one on your nose has disappeared. And look!" she added, picking something out of the basin. "Here's your left slipper."

Ellen said nothing, but she smiled as she put the slipper on.

She knew that it wasn't really her slipper. It belonged to Princess Mirror-Belle.